This Igloo book belongs to:

. . . .

igloo

Published in 2011
by Igloo Books Ltd
Cottage Farm
Sywell
NN6 0BJ
www.igloo-books.com

Copyright © 2010 Igloo Books Ltd

B044 1111
10 9 8 7 6 5 4 3
ISBN 978-0-85734-513-4

Illustrated by: Beverlie Manson, Diana Catchpole,
Roberta Collier, Dana Regan and Liza Woodruff
Stories retold by: Joff Brown

Printed and manufactured in China

Bedtime Stories for Girls

igloo

Contents

Little Red Riding Hood

Once upon a time, a little girl lived in a cottage with her mother, near the edge of a big, dark wood. She had a lovely, bright red cape with a hood and the little girl wore it so often, everyone called her, 'Little Red Riding Hood'.

One day, news reached the cottage that Little Red Riding Hood's grandmother was ill. So, her mother gave her a basket of delicious cakes to take to Granny. "Now, listen carefully," said Little Red Riding Hood's mother. "Remember to stay on the path that goes through the woods. You must not stop to pick flowers and don't talk to any strangers on the way."

The woods were deep and dark, even in the middle of the day, but Little Red Riding Hood wasn't scared. Even though she could see the beautiful flowers that grew along the side of the path, she obeyed her mother and did not stop to pick any of them. What Little Red Riding Hood did not know was that, deep in the shadowy trees, a wolf was watching her.

The wolf slunk out of the trees, swishing its bushy tail. "Who are you and where are you going, little girl?" he said.

Little Red Riding Hood had never seen a wolf before, so she wasn't scared. She forgot what her mother had told her about talking to strangers. "My name is Little Red Riding Hood," she said. "I'm off to visit my grandmother who lives on the other side of the wood."

"Really? How very interesting," said the wolf. "You should pick your grandmother some pretty flowers." "But my mother told me to stay on the path," said Little Red Riding Hood.

"It's very rude to go visiting someone without any flowers," said the wolf. "Anyway, I must be going now, goodbye." With that the wolf slunk off, back into the forest, as if he had never been there at all.

"How strange," thought Little Red Riding Hood. She continued on her way, but she couldn't help thinking about what the wolf had said. "Maybe Granny would like some flowers," she thought.

Further along the path, Little Red Riding Hood noticed some particularly pretty blooms. She couldn't resist any longer and left the path to pick some to give to her grandmother.

There were so many beautiful flowers to choose from, Little Red Riding Hood didn't realize how much time it was taking her. A long time passed before she had collected a perfect bouquet

"Hello," said a voice. It made Little Red Riding Hood jump. She turned to see a woodcutter, who was carrying an axe. "It's getting late," said the woodcutter. "You shouldn't be on your own in the wood."

Little Red Riding Hood told the woodcutter all about her journey. "Best be on your way then," he said, kindly. "Your grandmother will be waiting for you."

Meanwhile, the wolf had run all the way to Little Red Riding Hood's grandmother's house. He knocked on the door and spoke with a high, girlish voice. "Hello, Granny, it's Little Red Riding Hood, can I come in?"

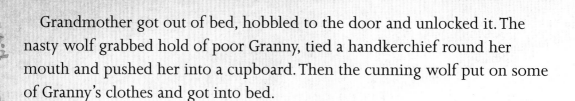

Grandmother got out of bed, hobbled to the door and unlocked it. The nasty wolf grabbed hold of poor Granny, tied a handkerchief round her mouth and pushed her into a cupboard. Then the cunning wolf put on some of Granny's clothes and got into bed.

A while later, Little Red Riding Hood finally reached her grandmother's house. She knocked on the door. "Hello, Granny, it's Little Red Riding Hood, can I come in?"
"Yes, of course, my child," said the wolf, in his best grandmother's voice.

Little Red Riding Hood came in and went over to the bed. "You must excuse my voice," said the wolf, with the sheets drawn right up to his chin. "I've been so ill, it's made me quite hoarse. Come over here and sit on the bed, my dear."

Little Red Riding Hood sat on the bed and looked at the wolf.
"Oh, Granny, what big ears you have," she said.
"All the better to hear you with," said the wolf.

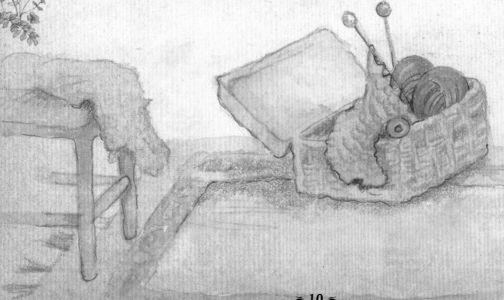

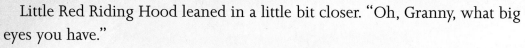

Little Red Riding Hood leaned in a little bit closer. "Oh, Granny, what big eyes you have."
"All the better to see you with," said the wolf.

Little Red Riding Hood began to feel there was something wrong. She looked at the wolf's paws holding the sheet. "Oh, Granny, what big hands you have."
"All the better to hug you with," said the wolf.

Little Red Riding Hood leaned in closer still, to get a better look. "Oh, Granny, what big teeth you have."
"All the better to EAT you with!" cried the wolf, as he sprang out of the bed.

But Little Red Riding Hood was a lot faster than her poor grandmother and she jumped out of the way just in time. The wolf chased her round and round the room. Suddenly, there was a knock at the door. Little Red Riding Hood ran over and flung the door open. Outside, stood the woodcutter.

The woodcutter had decided to check on Little Red Riding Hood and her grandmother, to make sure that they were safe. The moment he saw the wolf, the woodcutter swung his axe and chased the nasty creature out of the house and into the dark wood. The wolf got such a fright, he ran away and never came back again.

Little Red Riding Hood let her poor old granny out of the cupboard. Granny, the woodcutter and Little Red Riding Hood ate some of the delicious cakes from the basket. After that, Little Red Riding Hood promised never to stray from the path, ever again.

The Weather Witch

Peter and Polly lived in a little village surrounded by bright golden cornfields. Each year, the people of the village harvested the corn and milled it in the old windmill by the brook.

One summer, no rain came and the crops stopped growing. Peter and Polly asked their father what would happen. "If it does not rain, the seeds will not grow," their father said. "There will be no harvest and we shall starve. Some might say it is time to call on the Weather Witch."

Peter and Polly wanted to know all about the Weather Witch, so their father told them. "The tale of the Weather Witch is one that is told to children when the harvest fails, so listen carefully.

No one has ever seen The Weather Witch, but it is said that she controls the wind and the rain. She sends storms when she is angry and soft rain when she is at peace. I have heard folk say that she lives in a cave under a waterfall, many days journey from here."

The very next day, Peter and Polly set out to find the Weather Witch. They were walking through a field when they saw a cat with a field mouse in its paws. "Help me!" cried the mouse, "or I'll be eaten!"

Peter scared the cat away and the mouse thanked them. "I have no gold, or silver," said the mouse, "but maybe I can help you, too, one day."

Peter and Polly journeyed further, until their small supply of food was almost gone. Deep in a forest, they came upon a pigeon. It was lying on the floor, faint with hunger. "Please, can you spare me a crumb of food?" asked the pigeon.

Polly gave the pigeon her last bite of bread. Before long, the pigeon was strong enough to fly away. "I have no gold, or silver," said the pigeon, but maybe I can help you, too, one day."

That night, the two children slept on the cold forest ground. Something tickled Peter's nose and woke him up. It was a big, shiny green beetle and Peter went to brush the beetle off, but it said, "Please, don't turn me away. It's very cold out here. Can I sleep next to you tonight?"

Peter didn't like the idea of sleeping next to a beetle, but he was too kind-hearted to refuse and he let the little creature settle next to him.

In the morning, the beetle thanked Peter and said, "I have no gold, or silver, but maybe I can help you, too, one day."

Peter and Polly continued on their way and reached a waterfall, streaming into a wild river. Behind the waterfall was a dark cave. A fierce wind blew from the cave and, in the shadows, hunched and ragged, sat the Weather Witch. "What do you want?" she said, grumpily.

The children tried to hide their fear and told the witch that they needed rain for their harvest. The Weather Witch laughed and it sounded like a crack of thunder. "I will send rain to your village if you bring me three impossible things – a stone that sings, a pair of fairy's shoes and a living jewel. She cackled loudly and went into the darkness of her cave.

Peter and Polly thought about the Weather Witch's words. "What she asks is impossible," said Peter. "It's hopeless," sighed Polly. Suddenly, Peter felt something tugging at his sleeve. It was the mouse that they had rescued from the cat.

"I can help you," said the mouse. It scampered off, then returned with something in its paws. It was a stone with a hole in the middle. The children took the stone to the Weather Witch. When they held it up, the cold wind blew through it and it made a long, low whistling sound.

"A stone that sings!" said witch. "You have done well. But what about my fairy shoes?" And she sent the children back outside, where they sat wondering how they could possibly get some fairy shoes.

Just then, Polly felt something land on her shoulder. It was the pigeon they had fed earlier. "I can help you," it said. "Follow me, but be very quiet." So the children followed the pigeon to a secret grove, where they hid. Before long, when all was quiet, some fairies appeared.

The fairies danced and danced and then they fell asleep. The pigeon flew softly to them and removed a tiny pair of fairy shoes. "Don't worry, I'll return them afterwards," said the pigeon to the delighted children.

Peter and Polly rushed back to the cave and gave the fairy shoes to the Weather Witch, who scowled when she saw the second part of her task completed. "What about my living jewel?" she cried, creating an especially cold blast of wind and tossing the shoes out of the cave.

The children sat outside the cave thinking. This time, the big green beetle crawled up to them. "I would love to help you," it said, "but I have no secrets and no skill."

"Wait," said Polly. "You are the brightest green I have ever seen. You look just like a living jewel." They took the beetle into the cave, where the wind was roaring even more strongly than before. They showed the bright, shiny green beetle to the Weather Witch.

The Weather Witch took the beetle. She started to shake and make a deep, booming sound. The children got ready to run away, but then they realised that she was laughing. "You children are very clever!" chortled the Weather Witch. She handed them a glass ball. "Return to your village and break this ball."

When Peter and Polly reached their village after many days' travel, nobody believed them when they told their tale. Then the children threw the glass ball onto the ground, breaking it. Great, grey clouds spilled from the broken ball, filling the sky and a gentle rain began to fall.

"It's true!" said their father, hugging them both. That year, the crops grew higher than ever. The villagers had more than enough bread to eat and Peter and Polly lived happily ever after.

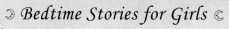

Goldilocks and the Three Bears

Once upon a time, there were three bears who lived in a cottage in the woods. There was Father Bear, Mother Bear and Baby Bear. One day, Mother Bear made porridge for breakfast, but it was too hot to eat, so the bears decided to go for a walk until it cooled down.

Meanwhile, a little girl called Goldilocks was walking in the woods. It wasn't long before Goldilocks realised that she was lost. She wandered through the forest, trying to find her way home, but soon she became cold and hungry.

Goldilocks was feeling very fed up when she came upon the three bears' cottage. "Maybe someone lives here who can help me," she said. She went up to the little cottage and knocked on the door, but nobody answered. Goldilocks peered into a window, but she couldn't see anybody inside. So she tried the door and found it was unlocked.

Goldilocks stepped inside the cottage. "Is anybody home?" she asked, but there was no reply because the three bears were still out on their morning walk. Goldilocks went to the kitchen and saw three bowls of porridge on the table. "I'm so hungry, I'm sure nobody will mind if I just have a taste," she thought to herself.

Goldilocks tasted the biggest bowl of porridge, but it was too hot.

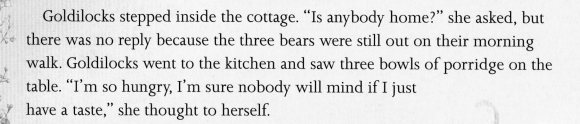

So she tasted the middle bowl of porridge, but it was too cold.

Then Goldilocks tasted the smallest bowl of porridge and it was just right. So she gobbled it all up.

When Goldilocks had finished the porridge, her tummy felt really full. "I think I will find somewhere comfortable to sit down and have a rest," she said.

Goldilocks looked around and saw three chairs. The first chair was very big and Goldilocks found it hard to climb up onto the seat.

So, she tried the middle chair instead. It was a bit better, but it was still too high.

However, when Goldilocks tried the smallest chair, it seemed to be just right

Goldilocks sat back on the chair and was just getting comfortable when suddenly, the legs snapped and she fell to the floor.

"I'm sleepy," thought Goldilocks, so she went upstairs and found a bedroom with three beds in it. There was a big one, a medium-sized one, and a tiny little one.

Goldilocks jumped onto the biggest bed, but it was far too hard.

So, she tried sleeping on the middle-sized bed, but it was far too soft.

Goldilocks laid down on the smallest bed. It was just right, so she laid her head on the pillow and fell fast asleep.

Soon, the three bears finished their walk and returned to the cottage. They were surprised to see that the front door was open. They went into the kitchen and Father Bear looked at the big bowl. "Someone's been eating my porridge," he said.

Mother Bear looked at the middle bowl, which had a spoon sticking out of it. "Someone's been eating my porridge," she said.

Baby Bear looked at the small bowl. "Someone's been eating MY porridge," he said, "and they've eaten it all up!"

Father Bear went to sit down, but the big chair wasn't in its usual place. "Someone's been sitting in my chair," he said.

Mother Bear saw that the middle chair had been moved, too. "Someone's been sitting in my chair," she said.

Baby Bear looked at the small chair lying smashed on the floor. "Someone's been sitting in MY chair," he wailed, "and they've broken it to pieces!" Baby Bear started to cry.

The three bears went upstairs to their bedroom. Father Bear saw that the sheets had fallen off the biggest bed. "Someone's been sleeping in my bed," he said.

Mother Bear looked at the crumpled pillows on the medium-sized bed. "Someone's been sleeping in my bed," she said.

Baby Bear pointed at the smallest bed. "Someone's been sleeping in MY bed," he said, "and she's still there!"

Suddenly, Goldilocks woke up with a start. She sat up and saw the three bears looking down at her. With a shriek, she scrambled out of the bed, ran downstairs and out of the cottage, into the woods. She didn't dare look behind her, in case the three bears were following her. But the three bears were still in the bedroom, scratching their heads and wondering why a little golden-haired girl had gone to sleep in Baby Bear's bed.

Goldilocks ran so fast, she soon found herself back home again. She rushed in and hugged her mother who had been worrying where she was. After that, Goldilocks didn't go into the woods by herself and she never went back to the three bears' cottage again.

The Tin Whistle

O nce upon a time, there was a princess who lived in an old, grey castle. Everyone but the princess who lived in there was sad. Even the king and queen were gloomy.

The castle was filled with dusty old furniture, suits of armour and paintings of unhappy-looking ancestors. The princess found it quite funny, in fact, she was the only cheerful one in the castle. However, try as she might, the princess could never raise anyone's spirits.

Sometimes, the princess would go for a walk in her favourite part of the garden. There, in a quiet corner, was a statue of a handsome young man, dressed as a prince. The young man's face had a very sad expression and the princess often wondered what had made him so unhappy.

One day, the princess was playing near the statue when she saw something shining in its stone hand. She climbed up and found a small, golden key. "I'm sure this wasn't here before," thought the princess. "I wonder what sort of lock a key like this opens?"

The princess searched all over the gloomy castle, from the cellars to the roof. Then, in the attic, she found a chest made of ancient wood. The princess put the key in the lock and, when she turned it, the lock clicked open. Inside the chest was an old tin whistle.

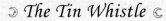

The princess took the tin whistle to her room and tried to play it. She was surprised to find that her fingers flew over the holes and she was able to play a lovely tune. The princess stood up and danced round and round her room as she played.

Suddenly, as if by magic, the china ornaments in the princess' room started to twirl and dance along to the music. The princess was very surprised, but she didn't stop playing.

The princess danced down the stairs, playing the tune. The rusty suits of armour came to life and marched merrily behind her. Even the knives and forks in the kitchen began to beat in time to the music. Then the plates and cups began to dance together.

In the great hall, all the chairs danced in formation and even the long, oak table began to jig around. Inside the paintings, the princess' ancestors danced and twirled. Even the stuffed moose head on the wall began to sing along, cheerfully.

"What is this noise?" asked the king, as he came marching into the hall with the queen. He grabbed the tin whistle and suddenly, all the dancing stopped. The king put the whistle in a drawer. "We'll have none of this in my castle," he said and sent the princess off to bed.

That night, the princess had a dream that she was looking out of her bedroom window at the statue in the garden. The statue seemed to be pleading with her. "Set me free," it said. "If you do not wake me tonight, I will remain stone for another one hundred years."

The princess woke up, dressed quietly and then crept downstairs. The castle guards were dozing and she slipped past them without a sound. The princess found the tin whistle in the drawer, where the king had put it, then she crept out into the moonlit garden.

Everything was still and quiet. The princess walked along the paths, towards the quiet spot, where the statue stood. She played softly on the tin whistle. The moonlight shone brighter and brighter on the statue of the young man and made it glow. The princess played faster and faster, until her fingers ached and she could hardly breathe.

Suddenly, the statue moved. It raised its hands and slowly, all the stone changed into living flesh. The young man stepped down from the statue and took the princess' hand.

"You have saved me," he said. "I am a prince who visited this castle one hundred years ago, to marry a princess. However, the princess' wicked and jealous stepmother cursed me to become a statue and for the castle to be forever gloomy. My only hope was that someone would find my magic whistle and use it to bring me back to life. Now the curse is broken."

As the sun came up, the castle came to life. The princess played the tin whistle and everything in the castle danced around. The prince and the princess went into the great hall to greet the king and queen.

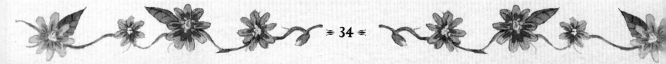

The king and queen weren't unhappy anymore. In fact, they were overjoyed to see their daughter and the prince. They smiled and hugged each other. "We have lived under this enchantment for far too long," they said. "Now that the curse has been broken, we will make this castle a happy place once more."

The prince fell in love with the princess and it wasn't long before they were married. On the day of their wedding, everyone in the castle danced and danced. The castle was filled with light and laughter and no one had any reason to be unhappy, ever again.

The Ugly Duckling

Once upon a time, in the shady reeds by a river bank, a mother duck sat on top of her eggs. She had been waiting a long while for them to hatch and was getting impatient. Soon, there were cracking sounds, as little ducklings emerged from their shells. One by one, the eggs hatched, except for one. The remaining egg was much larger than the rest and its shell was grey.

Finally, the big egg cracked and a duckling emerged. It didn't look at all like the other fluffy little ducklings. It was big and clumsy and instead of being a beautiful yellow color, it was a dirty grey. It had wide feet and a long neck. Even the mother duck didn't like the look of it.

When the other birds in the farmyard saw the big duckling, they laughed and laughed. "It's the ugliest duckling we've ever seen!" they said. The mother duck and her little ducklings agreed that the strange duckling was just too ugly to have around. The hens pecked him and the turkeys chased him. No one loved the poor little ugly duckling.

One day, the ugly duckling was so fed up that he decided to leave the farmyard and find some new friends. He waddled down to the river, where some wild ducks had landed. "Perhaps they will accept me," the duckling thought and he swam over to them.

Suddenly, there was a loud cracking noise. Before the ugly duckling could speak to the ducks, they flew away in fright. Nearby, hunters fired their guns. They were looking for birds to shoot and their hunting dog was crashing through the reeds. "He'll eat me up!" thought the terrified duckling. But the dog ran right past him.

"I'm even too ugly for a dog to eat!" thought the duckling.
He hid in the reeds, with his head bowed, waiting for the hunters to pass.

The ugly duckling swam down the river, until it reached a little cottage near the river bank. The door of the cottage opened and a stern-faced old woman came out, followed by a red hen and a black and white cat. The woman saw the ugly duckling and grabbed hold of it. "Look Hen, look, Cat," she said. "Now I shall have duck eggs for my supper."

Days passed, but the duckling didn't lay any eggs. "What use are you if you can't lay eggs?" said the hen.
"Can you purr, or catch mice, or arch your back, like me?" asked the cat.
"No, I can't," admitted the little duckling.
"Then you're useless!" said the cat and the hen agreed.

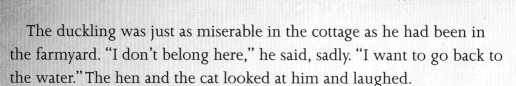

The duckling was just as miserable in the cottage as he had been in the farmyard. "I don't belong here," he said, sadly. "I want to go back to the water." The hen and the cat looked at him and laughed. "What a stupid idea," said the hen, clucking her disapproval. "You really are a very silly bird," added the cat.

One day, when no one was around, the duckling waddled outside and swam off down the river again. In the distance, he saw some beautiful swans flying across the sky. The ugly duckling had never seen such magnificent birds and his heart rose at the sight of them. "I wish I could be with them," he thought sadly. But they would never want to spend time with someone as ugly as me. I wish I were as lovely as they are."

Winter came and the weather became colder. The ugly duckling sat in the reeds, shivering and alone. The days and nights grew colder and colder until, eventually, the water froze over.

While sleeping one day, the ugly duckling was grabbed by a farmer and taken into his house. "This will make a good pet for my children," said the farmer and he put the duckling on some straw by the fire.

However, even though the farmer's house was warm and dry, the ugly duckling wasn't happy. The farmer's children teased him and chased him around the house. He flapped his wings to escape and knocked over a jug of milk, then he toppled over a basket of eggs on the table. The farmer was so cross, he threw the duckling out of the house.

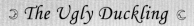

The poor little duckling had nowhere to go, so he hid in the reeds and waited for the long, dark months of winter to pass. Snow and ice covered the land and everything was frozen.

Very slowly, winter turned into spring and the little duckling felt warm rays of sunshine on his back. The ice began to thaw and the snow began to melt. Once again, the river flowed and the duckling was able to swim. Now, however, he found that he could swim faster than before. He had grown too, and his feathers had changed color.

One day, the beautiful swans flew down and landed on the river. Even though he was scared of being pecked and laughed at, the duckling decided to speak to the birds. "I don't care if they laugh at me," he thought.

The duckling swam up to the swans. "I'm just an ugly duckling," he said, sadly. "Please don't laugh at me or peck me, I only want to speak to you,"

The swans looked at each other in amazement. "Look down into the water," said one swan, softly. The ugly duckling looked down at its reflection for the first time that spring. Instead of a gawky, grey bird, it was amazed to find a beautiful white swan staring back at it.

"I'm a swan!" he cried and curved his long, slender neck in joy. The other swans were very happy to have met their new friend. "Fly with us, brother," they said and they all took off into the sky.

The ugly duckling had changed into a beautiful swan. His time of unhappiness and misfortune was over and, at last, he had found his true brothers and sisters. The swan lived a long and happy life and was never lonely again.

The Emperor's New Clothes

A long time ago, there lived an emperor who loved clothes more than anything else. Instead of trying to care for his people, he spent all the kingdom's money on fine, new garments. And there was nothing the emperor liked more than parading his new clothes in front of everyone, so they could say how elegant he looked.

One day, two cunning thieves arrived at the emperor's palace. "This silly emperor loves clothes so much," they agreed, "it will be easy to make him shower us with gold." So the thieves went to the emperor and introduced themselves. "We are the finest tailors in the world," they said. "We will make you the best suit of clothes that there has ever been."

At first, the emperor didn't believe them. "I have seen all the finest clothes the world has to offer," he said. "What can you two do that is better than what I have seen already?"

"We have a roll of magic cloth," they said. "It has the finest colors and patterns you have ever seen. It is so exquisite that only the cleverest, most refined people can see it. It is invisible to anyone who is incredibly stupid, or who does not deserve to be doing his job."

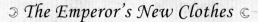 

"That sounds marvellous," said the emperor, clapping his hands. "If I have a suit of this material, I will know exactly which of my ministers deserves his job and I can make sure I am not surrounded by stupid people."

The thieves looked at each other and smiled. "The magic material is very expensive to make," said one thief. "I'm not sure your excellency can afford it," said the other.

"Nonsense!" shouted the emperor. "Here, take a thousand gold coins, that should be more than enough to make the suit."

The thieves left the palace with the money and used it to buy two huge looms for weaving cloth. But, because they had made up the story of the cloth, there was nothing to weave.

For weeks and weeks, the swindlers spent their money on whatever they liked and did no work at all. Then, one day, there was a knock on their door. It was the emperor and all his men. "We have come to see how my suit is progressing," said the emperor.

The two thieves turned the handles of the looms with nothing on them, and cut through the air with scissors. "See, Your Excellency," they said. "Isn't it the most marvellous cloth you have ever seen?"

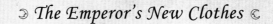

The emperor was shocked. He couldn't see any cloth at all. "Oh, no!" he thought. "It's just as I always thought. I'm either too stupid to see the cloth, or I don't deserve to be emperor. Nobody must ever know, or they would never let me rule." So he said to the thieves, "Yes, of course, it's certainly the finest cloth I have ever seen."

The thieves showed the imaginary cloth to the emperor's court, too. Each of them thought the same thing, "I must be too stupid, or unworthy, to see the cloth. I will pretend I can see it, so that the emperor does not punish me."

All the emperor's men pointed and applauded and said how fine the cloth was. "Of course, we'll need another thousand gold coins to finish it off," said the thieves. "After all, you wouldn't want to go outside with it half-finished like this." So, the emperor gave them the money without delay.

Many more weeks passed and the thieves returned to the palace. "We have finished the suit of clothes for you, Your Excellency," they said. They took the emperor into his rooms and pretended to fit the clothes on top of his under garments. "The cloth is so very fine and light, that only those with the most delicate skin can feel it," the thieves said. The emperor couldn't feel anything, of course, but he didn't want to look coarse and rough. "Oh, yes," he said. "It feels lighter than air."

When they were done, the thieves stood back and looked at the emperor, who was wearing nothing at all. "Our finest work!" the thieves said. "You are a marvel of modern fashion."

The emperor summoned his courtiers and they walked through the streets of the city. Everyone had heard of the magic cloth. To make sure nobody thought they were stupid, they all pretended that they could see the emperor's new clothes.

The procession wound its way through every street, even the very poorest ones. As they were passing one tiny house, a little girl and her father came out to watch them go past. The child hadn't heard about the magic cloth. "Look, Daddy," she said, "that funny man has come out in his underwear."

The child's father saw that his daughter was right. "You speak the truth, my dear," he said, laughing. "The emperor has no new clothes!"

The family next door heard the man and knew that what he said was true. "The emperor has no new clothes," they shouted. The message passed quickly from door to door and from street to street, until everyone in the city was pointing and laughing at the emperor. "The emperor has no new clothes!" they cried.

Finally, the emperor understood that what everyone was saying was true. At first, he was so embarrassed, he couldn't speak. But then, he too began to laugh, until he thought his sides would split. "I have been a proud and foolish man," he said to everyone, "and I have learned my lesson."

The thieves had fled the city and were never seen there again, but the emperor became a good and wise ruler who cared more about his people than his pride. And so the emperor and his people lived happily ever after.

The Three Little Pigs

Once upon a time, there were three little pigs who wanted to leave home. "We must build our own houses," they said. The three little pigs said goodbye to their mother and set off.

The first little pig hadn't walked very far when he met a man carrying a bale of straw. The little pig bought the bale of straw and started to build a house. When he was finished, the first little pig had a house of straw. It had a straw door, straw walls and straw windows.

The second little pig met a man carrying a great bundle of sticks. The little pig bought the sticks and made himself a house of sticks. It was stronger than the house of straw and the second little pig was very proud of it.

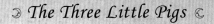

The third little pig walked a long way and came upon a man carrying lots of bricks. The little pig bought the bricks and built himself a house that was very strong and sturdy.

The little pigs didn't know it, but they were being watched by a hungry wolf, who loved to eat little pigs. He went to the house of straw and knocked on the door.

"Little pig, little pig, let me come in," said the wolf.
"Not by the hair on my chinny-chin-chin!" said the first little pig.
"Then I'll huff and I'll puff and I'll blow your house down!" cried the wolf.
And he huffed and he puffed and he blew the straw house down.

The poor little pig squealed and ran all the way to his brother's house made of sticks. He ran inside, just before the wolf knocked on the door.

"Little pig, little pig, let me come in," growled the wolf.
"Not by the hair on my chinny-chin-chin!" said the second little pig.
"Then I'll huff and I'll puff and I'll blow your house down!" said the wolf.
And he huffed and he puffed and he blew the little stick house down.

The two little pigs ran as fast as they could to the house of the third little pig. As soon as they were inside and had bolted the door, they heard a loud knocking.

"Little pig, little pig, let me come in!" said the wolf.
"Not by the hair on my chinny-chin-chin!" said the third little pig.
"Then I'll huff and I'll puff and I'll blow your house down!" said the wolf.
So he huffed and he puffed, but nothing happened!

The wolf huffed and puffed again, but still nothing happened. The third little pig's house of bricks was too sturdy and the wolf couldn't blow it down.

The wolf was out of breath, but hungrier than ever. "I'll have to trick those pigs into leaving the house," he thought. So, the wolf put on his kindest voice and tapped on the door. "You will get hungry soon, little piggies and I don't mean you any harm. Won't you come and pick some turnips with me tomorrow, at six o'clock?"

Now, the third little pig knew that the wolf wanted to eat him and his brothers, so he thought of a way to outwit him. "We'd love to pick turnips with you," he said. "Please call again tomorrow, at six o'clock."

The next day, the three little pigs tiptoed out of the house at five o'clock. They gathered all the turnips from the nearby field. Then they tiptoed back to the house. At six o'clock, the wolf knocked on the door. "Time to get turnips, little piggies!" he growled, softly.

"You're late!" shouted the third little pig. "Sorry, but we've already got the turnips!" Inside the brick house, the three little pigs were all laughing at the wolf.

The wolf was very cross, but he wasn't about to be beaten by three silly, little pigs, so he thought of another plan. "There are some juicy apples in the orchard nearby. Come with me tomorrow, at five o'clock, and I will help you pick some," he said. The little pigs agreed to meet the wolf, but first, they set about making a big pot of boiling turnip soup.
"This will come in very handy," said the third little pig.

The next day, the little pigs tiptoed out of the house at four o'clock and ran to the orchard. "We will make a fool of that silly, old wolf," they giggled, as they picked the juicy, green apples.

But the wily wolf had guessed what the pigs were up to and he went to the orchard early, too. He found the three little pigs with a big basket of apples, all ready to go home. He growled and chased them out of the orchard, all the way back to the brick house, but the pigs got inside just in time.

Now the wolf was really angry. He snarled and jumped onto the roof of the little brick house. "Little pigs," he growled, "I'm going to eat you all up!" Then he jumped down the chimney.

☙ The Three Little Pigs ☙

But the wolf didn't know that, at the bottom of the chimney, was the pot of turnip soup. He fell into it with a great big SPLASH and got such a fright, he ran away and never bothered the little pigs ever again.

The three little pigs were very happy to be free of the big, bad, wolf. The third little pig built his two brothers brand new houses made of bricks, just like his own — and they all lived safely and happily ever after.

The Tortoise and the Hare

One fine day in spring, the animals of the meadow were playing in the sunshine, when a slick, speedy hare bounded up to them. The hare was very proud of how fast he could run and wanted to show off to all the other animals. He ran round the old bear from the woods, raced past the rabbits and out-ran the swift, sly fox.

"I'm the fastest creature in the world," said the hare, proudly. "No one can beat me." He kicked his heels up and raced round and round, so that all the animals could see him, then he stood on the meadow path and smiled smugly.

The hare was just thinking about how marvellous he was, when a small voice spoke behind him. Turning around, the hare saw an old tortoise. His shell was worn with age and he used a gnarled old twig as a walking stick. "Excuse me," said the tortoise. "Would you mind moving out of the way? My old legs aren't what they used to be."

The hare looked the old tortoise up and down. "I am the fastest animal in the world," he said. "Why should I move out of the way for a slow, old tortoise, like you?"

The tortoise thought for a minute. "If you won't move," he croaked, narrowing his dark eyes, "perhaps you'd like to have a race?"
The hare laughed so much, he nearly fell over. "I would cross the finishing line before you even took your first step," he said.

"Nevertheless," said the tortoise, nodding. "I suggest we race up the old hill. The animal that reaches the top first, will be forever known as the fastest animal in the world."

"Agreed!" said the hare. Then, without waiting for another word from the tortoise, the hare sped off in the direction of the hill.

The hare ran faster than ever, across the green meadow. Before long, he had reached the steep slopes of the hill and began to bound up them. The hare looked behind him, but couldn't see the tortoise. "How will he know I'm winning?" he thought. "I have so much time, I'm going to go back and tell that tortoise how fast I am!" With that, the hare raced back down the hill.

Right near the start of the race, the tortoise was still plodding slowly along. "Ha!" panted the hare. "I am so fast that I have come back to tell you that I almost reached the top of the hill."

"Almost reaching the top of the hill doesn't make you a winner," wheezed the old tortoise, and he continued to plod along, one, slow step at a time.

The hare raced back to the hill. He was so sure of his success that he started leaping high in the air. "If I do this, that silly old tortoise is bound to see how far ahead I am," said the hare. He even stopped to tell all the woodland creatures about the race. "I have so much time," said the hare, "I can do whatever I want and still win!"

The Tortoise and the Hare

The hare spent so much time showing off to all the other animals, that he was beginning to feel tired. He tried to bound up the hill, but this time, because the hare had been running all day, it wasn't so easy.

The proud hare refused to climb the hill slowly. "I'm the fastest animal in the world," he thought. "I can run straight up this hill." Instead of climbing the hill bit by bit, the hare charged upwards, using up most of his energy. When he finally reached the top, he was exhausted. Just up ahead was the tree that marked the finishing line.

"I'm so tired," yawned the hare. He looked down the hill, but the old tortoise was nowhere to be seen. "I'm still so far ahead, it can't hurt to take a little nap," he said, sleepily. So the hare lay down on the cool grass and fell fast asleep.

Meanwhile, the old tortoise plodded on and on, never speeding up, but never slowing down, either. He just kept going at his own tortoise pace.

At the top of the hill, the hare slept for hours and hours. When he woke, the sun was almost setting. "How silly of me," said the hare, yawning and rubbing his eyes. "I've got a race to win."

The hare looked up towards the tree at the top of the hill and couldn't believe his eyes. The tortoise was about to cross the finishing line.

Determined not to be beaten by an old, slow tortoise, the hare shot off like a flash towards the tree. It tore through the grass, jumped through the ferns, then tripped and fell headfirst into a thorn bush. The hare rolled out of the thorn bush and scrambled across to the tree - only to find that it was too late. The tortoise had won the race!

A crowd of cheering animals surrounded the tortoise. "Well done," said the badger, "you are the winner of this race and therefore, the fastest animal in the world."

When the hare heard this, he stared with his mouth open. Then he began to laugh. Soon the tortoise was laughing too and before long, all the other animals joined in. "I'm sorry I was so rude to you," said the hare to the tortoise. "I was so busy showing off and telling everyone how fast I was, I used up all my energy. But you just kept going and going – and you won the race, fair and square."

The tortoise smiled wisely. "Sometimes, slow and steady is best," he said. The hare agreed and from that day on, he became a lot less boastful and proud. Whenever he felt the need to show off, the hare remembered how the tortoise had won the race.

As for the tortoise, it took him a long time to plod all the way home, but he smiled every slow step of the way.

Hansel and Gretel

Once upon a time, there was a boy named Hansel and his sister, Gretel. They lived with their father and their stepmother in a little house deep in the forest. The family were poor and there were many days when they had nothing to eat.

One night, the stepmother said to their father, "We have no food for the children. I will take them to my sister's house, where they will be better fed." However, the stepmother secretly wanted to get rid of Hansel and Gretel. She planned to take them in the forest and leave them there.

The next morning, the stepmother gave Hansel and Gretel some bread for their lunch and led them out into the woods. Hansel, who was clever, guessed that something was wrong. When the stepmother wasn't looking, he tore up his bread and scattered it behind him as they walked.

The stepmother made Hansel and Gretel walk a very long way. When they became tired, she told them to sleep under a tree. However, while the brother and sister were sleeping, the stepmother left and returned home.

When Hansel and Gretel woke up, they found they were all alone. It was cold and dark. "Don't worry," said Hansel. "All we have to do is follow my trail of bread crumbs back to our cottage."

But when they went to look for the trail, the children couldn't find it anywhere. The birds of the forest had eaten every single bread crumb, so Hansel and Gretel had no way to get back home.

Hours passed and the children became more and more lost. They had wandered deep into the forest, when they saw a little house in a clearing.

The house was strange and wonderful. Hansel and Gretel had never seen anything like it. The walls were made of gingerbread, the windows were gumdrops, the door was chocolate and the chimney was a big candy cane.

The brother and sister were so hungry that they rushed up to the house and broke off a large chunk of gingerbread. They ate it ravenously and it tasted delicious.

All of a sudden, the chocolate door flew open. An ugly old woman came rushing out. "You naughty children," she cried. "I'll teach you to eat my house." The woman grabbed Hansel and Gretel with her bony hands and dragged them inside, locking the chocolate door behind them.

The woman was a witch. She pushed Hansel into a cage that hung from the ceiling. "I'll be able to keep an eye on you up there," she said. Then the witch made Gretel do the cleaning. "You cannot go to bed until my house is spotless," she cackled. "However, if you do a good job, you will both get lots of sweets to eat."

Just as she promised, the witch gave Hansel and Gretel lots of sweets to eat. At first, the children liked it, but soon they felt sick from eating sweet, sticky sugar all day and they longed for a simple piece of bread.

Each day, the witch would feel Hansel's finger through the bars of his cage and mutter to herself, "Not yet, not yet." Then she would make Hansel eat even more sweets, but the witch never told either of the children why.

One night, Gretel heard the witch mumbling in her sleep. "Mmm, delicious! Hansel, for my supper!" Gretel realized why the witch was feeding Hansel so much candy. She was fattening him up so she could eat him for her dinner!

Gretel told Hansel about the evil plan. So, the next time the witch felt Hansel's finger through the bars, to see if he was fat enough to eat, Hansel stuck a twig out instead. The witch couldn't see very well, so she didn't notice. "Too skinny!" she croaked. "I won't eat you today!"

Even though the witch fed Hansel more and more sweets, he always held out the twig. "Your brother is very strange," said the witch to Gretel, one day. "However much he eats, he never gets any fatter. I think I'll roast him and gobble him up as a snack!"

The witch forced Gretel to light the huge old oven in the corner of the gingerbread house. Because Hansel wasn't fat enough for a proper supper, the witch decided to eat both children together. "Be a good girl and get in the oven and see if it's hot enough yet," said the witch, slyly. When Gretel was inside, the witch planned to close the door and roast her.

But Gretel was as clever as her brother. Instead of getting into the oven, she said, "That's funny. It doesn't seem to be warm at all." "Nonsense," said the witch. "Stand aside and let me see." And the witch climbed all the way into the hot oven.

Quick as a flash, Gretel slammed the door of the big oven and trapped the witch inside. She ran to Hansel and unlocked his cage. They were so happy to be back together again, they hugged each other as if they would never let go. "Quick!" said Gretel. "We must run!"

Before they left, Hansel went upstairs to the witch's room and searched it. Soon he found what he was looking for – a map of the forest. He ran back downstairs, flung open the chocolate door and the two children escaped.

With the help of the map, Hansel and Gretel soon found their way home. In their little house, they found their father crying. He had missed Hansel and Gretel so much. When they told him that the stepmother had abandoned them, their father sent her away forever. And Hansel, Gretel and their father lived happily ever after.

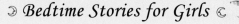

Rumpelstiltskin

Once upon a time, a king visited a humble miller. The miller longed to impress the king, so he boasted about his beautiful daughter. "My daughter is a very good spinner," said the miller. "She can spin straw into gold!"

The king was amazed to hear this. He ordered the miller's daughter to be locked in a tower in his castle. He left her there with a heap of straw and a spinning wheel. "You have three days to spin all this straw into gold," said the king. "If you fail, you will be punished."

But the poor miller's daughter couldn't really spin straw into gold. Her father had lied to the king and now she had been set an impossible task. The miller's daughter sat in the tower room and wept.

Suddenly, the stone wall of the tower seemed to ripple like water and a strange little man stepped through. He was short and had an ugly, bearded little face. "What's all this noise?" asked the man, grumpily. The miller's daughter explained her problem.

The little man stroked his hairy chin. "What will you give me if I spin this straw into gold?" he asked. The miller's daughter thought hard. "You can have my necklace," she said.

The man looked at the girl's necklace and nodded. He sat at the spinning wheel and began to spin. By morning, he had spun some of the straw into gold. Then, as quickly as he had arrived, the strange little man disappeared back into the wall.

The next morning, the king was pleased when he saw the gold, but he wanted more. "If the rest of the straw isn't spun into gold in two days, you will be punished," he said to the miller's daughter.

That night, the little man returned. "What will you give me if I spin you more gold?" he asked. The miller's daughter gave him her bracelet and the man spun more of the straw into gold.

When the king came to collect the gold the next morning, he was very happy. He thought the miller's daughter was beautiful and he almost told her to stop spinning, but he couldn't resist wanting more gold. "You must spin the remaining straw into gold tonight," he said.

That night, the miller's daughter waited and waited for the little man to appear. It was past midnight before the wall rippled and he stepped out. "Quick," she said. "You must spin the rest of the straw into gold, or I shall be in great trouble."

The little man grinned at her. "What will you give me if I do?" But the miller's daughter had nothing left to give to him.
"I will spin this straw into gold for you," said the man, "if you promise to give me your first-born child."

The miller's daughter was so frightened, she agreed. The little man sat at the wheel and worked faster than ever. Just as the sun came up, the last straw was spun into gold. The little man disappeared through the wall and the king opened the door.

The king was so amazed at the miller's daughter's skill and beauty that he asked her to marry him straight away. The miller's daughter agreed, as long as the king never asked her to spin gold into straw again.

The king was married to the miller's daughter and she became the queen. In time, she had a beautiful, baby daughter. She had forgotten all about her promise until one day, the wall of her room rippled like water and the strange little man stepped out. "You made a promise to give me your first-born child," he said.

The queen hugged her baby tight and would not let her go. "Take all my riches instead," she pleaded.

"No!" snapped the little man in triumph. "Only those who know my name have power over me. You do not know my name, so I will take your baby and you cannot stop me."

"Wait," said the queen, trying to think quickly. "It took you three days to spin the straw, so I should have three days to guess your name."

"Very well," said the little man. "But in three days, your baby is mine!"

The next day, when the man reappeared, the queen tried all the names she could think of. The little man just laughed and said, "no," to every one that she suggested.

On the second day, the queen searched through every book in the castle's great library. There was nothing about a little man who could spin straw into gold. Once again, the cackling man appeared and then disappeared when the queen failed to guess his name.

On the morning of the third day, the queen was in despair at not being able to figure out the man's name. She took her baby out with her and walked for miles, through fields and forests.

Just as the queen was ready to give up, she saw a thin line of smoke, floating through the trees. Following it, she saw a funny little house. Outside the house, there was a small fire. The little man who had spun gold from straw was dancing around the fire, laughing and singing a strange song.

The queen crouched down by the trees and kissed her baby to make sure she made no noise. Then she listened to the little man's song.
"The queen's daughter I'll surely claim.
The queen can't beat me at my game.
Rumplestiltskin is my name!"
The queen crept away and then rushed back to the castle, as fast as she could.

Later that night, just as he had done before, the strange little man appeared. "Your time is up," he said. The child is mine, so hand her over. I will take her to Fairyland and she will grow up to be my slave." The little man clapped his hands with glee.

"I have one last guess," said the queen. "I think that your name is Rumpelstiltskin."

When Rumpelstiltskin heard his name being spoken, he was enraged. His face was red with fury. He jumped up and down and stamped so hard on the ground, he made a great hole in it. Then he disappeared through the wall, still shouting and screaming with rage. After that, Rumpelstiltskin was never seen, or heard of again.

The king and queen's daughter grew up to be a beautiful young woman. No one ever told her that she was once nearly spirited off to Fairyland and everyone lived happily ever after.

The Magic Cake

Once there was a young princess who was greatly loved by all the servants in her palace. Although she was happy to spend time with her royal parents, the princess enjoyed sneaking away to visit the palace kitchens.

The chief cook was the princess' special friend. She was a big, round woman with twinkling eyes. Her hands were dusty with flour and her cheeks were always rosy red. The cook was cheerful most of the time, except when the greedy palace cats tried to steal food from her kitchen table. Then the cook would wave her rolling pin and chase them away.

Each day, the princess helped the cook make pies and pastries and sometimes she was allowed to lick the sticky spoon when the cook was making her famous cakes.

The princess' birthday was approaching, so she decided to invite all her friends to a big party to celebrate. It was going to be the social event of the season and the princess couldn't wait to eat her birthday cake.

One night, just before her birthday, the princess ran down the stairs to the big kitchen. But, when she opened the door, the princess got a surprise. The cook was waving her rolling pin like a magic wand. Around her, all the pots, pans and cutlery were jumping into the kitchen sink to clean themselves. Then they dried themselves and flew into the kitchen cupboards.

When the cook saw the princess, she made all the magic disappear with a wave of her rolling pin wand. "I'm an enchantress," explained the cook, "but, if people saw me use my powers, they might think I was a witch. So I only use them to clean the kitchen. If you agree to keep my secret, I will make you an extra-special birthday cake."

The princess agreed to keep the cook's secret. She would never have told on her friend, anyway. Still, she was very excited that she was going to get a special birthday cake.

The princess told all her friends about the extra-special cake. But, when her birthday arrived and all the guests went to sit at the table, the princess was disappointed to see a simple cake with nothing more than white icing and a few candles in the middle.

"How dull!" said some of the guests to each other and laughed. The princess wished she hadn't said anything to her friends. She cut the cake anyway and gave a slice to each of the guests.

As the princess was cutting a piece of cake for herself, she noticed a slip of paper stuck to the icing. It had a message from the cook which said, "More cake changes you back." The princess was very puzzled, but she took a big bite of the delicious cake and thought about what the note might mean.

Suddenly, the princess felt a tickle on her shoulders. Looking round, she saw that she had sprouted bright, feathery rainbow wings. When she looked around the table, she saw that all her guests were growing wings, too.

Next, the party guests began to shrink and became the size of fairies. Everyone squealed with excitement, as they realised they could fly.

"I knew the cake would be magic!" said the princess and she led her guests out into the palace corridors. They giggled and shrieked with delight, as they flew into every room, swooping and diving. They were like excited fairies, flitting here, there and everywhere.

After lots of zooming around the huge palace, the party guests began to feel tired. Flying was fun, but it was very hard work. "We can't keep our wings, forever," they said. "But how do we change back?"

The princess remembered the note from the cook. Now she understood what it meant. "We have to eat more cake," said the princess.

So, with a great fluttering of their rainbow wings, everyone flew back to the cake on the table. But the greedy palace cats had got there first. They were eating the cake and hissed at anyone who tried to stop them.

"If we don't eat more cake," said the princess, "we'll have to stay this size forever!" The princess swooped down towards the table. The cats swiped at her with their sharp claws, but she was too fast for them and grabbed a huge piece of cake.

As soon as the princess and the guests had eaten the cake, they lost their wings and grew to their full size again. Everyone was exhausted, but happy. "The was the best party ever!" said the guests.

The princess thanked the cook for her special cake. The cook promised that, at least once a year, on her birthday, the princess would always have some magic cake, so that she and her friends could fly like real fairies.

The Nightingale
and the North Wind

One windy evening, a little nightingale was singing her sweet, beautiful melody in a big horse-chestnut tree on a village green. The North Wind, the coldest and iciest of the four winds, blew so hard, it whistled through the leaves and shook the branches of the tree. The poor nightingale nearly fell off her branch and had to stop singing. "North Wind!" she cried. "Please stop all that blowing and whistling. I'm trying to sing."

The North Wind heard the nightingale. "Why should I, the mightiest of winds, stop blowing for you, little bird?" he asked.
"The answer to that question is a very simple one," said the nightingale. "You should stop blowing because my song is more powerful than your mighty breath.

The North Wind thought that this was most amusing. "Is that so?" he said. "In that case, would you care to make a bet?"
"Certainly," said the nightingale. "What are your terms?"

The North Wind thought for a moment. "We'll see who can make the most people in the village gather by this big tree," he said. "I'll go first and if I win, I will blow as hard as I like, forever. However, if you win, I agree to stop blowing altogether."

The nightingale agreed to the bet and flew off to a nearby bush to watch.

At first, the North Wind tried blowing the villagers who were out walking. However, even though he managed to blow a few of them towards the tree, most of the villagers were already inside, eating their dinner, or getting ready for bed. As soon as the North Wind turned to blow at one villager, another one would seize their chance and run back inside.

The North Wind blustered and grumbled and then he had another idea. He blew at the tree as hard as he could. The branches and their big, long leaves swayed in the wind. The North Wind blew even harder, until the weather vane on top of the church whirled like a spinning top.

The people of the village peeped out of their windows and wondered what was happening. "It's strange weather for this time of year," they said, as they watched the wind blow through the village.

The North Wind blew so hard that a great branch of the horse-chestnut tree broke with a giant crack. It fell down onto the ground in a shower of leaves. "Now everyone in the village will come out to see," said the North Wind.

Some of the villagers rushed out to look at the broken branch, scratching their heads and complaining to each other about the awful weather. However, most of them stayed inside, fearful of the giant gusts of wind.

"Half the village must be out here," said the North Wind to the nightingale. "I'd like to see you do better."
The nightingale just nodded. "Wait until tomorrow night." she cheeped, cheerfully.

By the next evening, the villagers had cleared away the branch, fixed the thatch back onto their roofs and everything was back to normal.
The nightingale chose a much lower branch than usual and began to sing her wonderful song.

At first, the village green was empty. The North Wind who was looking on, laughed. "You see, nightingale," he hissed. "All your singing can't match my mighty breath."

The nightingale ignored him and just carried on singing her sweet, beautiful song. Nearby, a little girl was going home with her mother. "Listen," said the girl. "What a beautiful sound."

Soon, the mother began to listen to the nightingale's song, too. A man came and joined them. "What are you doing?" he asked. Then the man heard the nightingale singing and he stopped to listen as well.

Soon, more people began to stop to hear the nightingale's song.
The people in their houses wondered why their neighbours were gathering round the horse-chestnut tree and came to look.

The nightingale sang as loud and as beautifully as she could. Before long, the whole village had gathered around the horse-chestnut tree in wonder and delight.

"You win," said the North Wind. "You may be small, but your song really is more powerful than my mighty breath."

After that, the North Wind never blew around the horse-chestnut tree again and the nightingale sang sweetly to the villagers for many, happy years.